To Eva,
Jakob, and Esmé

First U.S. edition 2012

Library of Congress Cataloging-in-Publication Data is available.

Library of Congress Catalog Card Number pending

ISBN 978-0-7636-5868-7

12 13 14 15 16 17 LEO 10 9 8 7 6 5 4 3 2 1

Printed in Heshan, Guangdong, China

This book was typeset in Berkeley Old Style. The illustrations were done in ink and watercolor.

Candlewick Press, 99 Dover Street, Somerville, Massachusetts 02144

visit us at www.candlewick.com

CANDLEWICK PRESS

Christmas at the TOY MUSEUM

David Lucas

It was Christmas Eve, and all the visitors to the Toy Museum were gone. The lights were out, the doors were locked, and all the toys hurried to the big Christmas tree.

But there weren't any presents!
None at all.
Nothing for Christmas for any of them.

But Bunting the old toy cat
had an idea.

He had to make a speech.
"Friends! Toys! Dolls! Puppets!"
he said. "It's Christmas Eve! Let us
not be downhearted! Why don't
we all give one another *ourselves*?"

It was an excellent speech,
and all the toys agreed it
was a wonderful idea.

And they all wrapped each other in turn . . .

until there was only Bunting left.

He climbed into a box
and shut his eyes tight.

All the toys stayed very still
and tried not to rustle or fidget.

At the top of the tree, lived an angel.
She wasn't a toy angel, she was a REAL angel.

And she thought it was so kind of the toys
to give themselves to one another.

But she knew what would happen
on Christmas morning.

Long hours passed in perfect silence.

At last, the toys *did* begin to fidget.

They couldn't help it.

They began to rustle and squeak and rattle and chatter.

"It *must* be Christmas morning now!" they said.

But how could they tell?

Bunting had his eyes shut tight.

"I think it must be," he said. "Who wants to go first?"

"Me!" said Banger the Boxer Dog,
and he sprang out of his wrapping.

And they all unwrapped
each other in turn . . .

until last of all, Peg the Peg Doll
unwrapped Bunting.

Bunting looked at all the other toys.
There was no one left for him to unwrap.
Bunting *still* didn't have a present
on Christmas.

High above, the angel smiled.
She had known this would happen,
so she spread her shining wings
and flew down from the top of the tree.

The toys gasped.

"Merry Christmas!" the angel said, and she handed Bunting a golden box tied with a golden ribbon.

And then she flew away.

"Open it! Open it!" said the toys all together.
Bunting pulled on the ribbon.
Out jumped a little glowing star,
dancing in the air.

"I am a WISH," said the star.
"A wish?" said Bunting.
He knew just what to wish for.

"I wish that Christmas Day
could last forever!" he said.

And it did.

MERRY